The Crazy Friend

by **Kim Kane**
illustrated by **Jon Davis**

PICTURE WINDOW BOOKS
a capstone imprint

For my old law school and not-in-the-least-bit-crazy
friend Tony Wilson, now a generous and talented
colleague. And for Martha, my 3-foot muse,
to whom Ginger owes every ounce of her vim.

— Kim

Ginger Green is published by Picture Window Books,
A Capstone Imprint
1710 Roe Crest Drive
North Mankato, Minnesota 56003
www.mycapstone.com

Ginger Green, Playdate Queen — *The Crazy Friend*
Text Copyright © 2016 Kim Kane
Illustration Copyright © 2016 Jon Davis
Series Design Copyright © 2016 Hardie Grant Egmont
First published in Australia by Hardie Grant Egmont 2016

Library of Congress Cataloging-in-Publication Data
is available on the Library of Congress website.

978-1-5158-1947-9 (library binding)
978-1-5158-1953-0 (paperback)
978-1-5158-2015-4 (eBook PDF)
978-1-5158-2033-8 (reflowable epub)

Summary: Ginger likes to play with Maisy, but when Maisy's bad behavior
makes a fun playdate turn bad, what can Ginger do to fix things?

Designers: Mack Lopez and Russell Griesmer
Production specialist: Tori Abraham

Printed and bound in China.
010737S18

Table of Contents

Chapter One

My name is Ginger Green.

I am seven years old.

I am the Playdate Queen!

This afternoon, I am having a playdate with my school friend Maisy.

M
T
W
T
F
S
S SUNDAY 2pm
—
MAISY
My House!!

Last night, I called Maisy on Mom's cell phone.

I said, "Maisy, this is Ginger Green, Playdate Queen. Would you like to come over tomorrow and play with me?"

Maisy screamed,

"YES!"

The doorbell rings at two o'clock.
It rings and rings.

"CUT IT OUT!"

yells my big sister, Violet.
"I am trying to read."

IINNNGG

"Cut it out!"

yells my little sister,
Penny.

Penny runs
to the door.

Penny is naked. Penny is always naked. She can't reach the handle.

"Pants on, Penny," says Mom.

"*Anything* on, Penny," I say.

Mom opens the door.

"Hi!" screams Maisy over the doorbell.

"Hi!" shouts Mom.

Maisy is still ringing the bell. I did not expect Maisy to be so noisy.

"Maisy is very excited," says Maisy's mom. "Bye, darling. See you at four o'clock."

Maisy's mom looks happy.
My mom does NOT.

"Stop ringing the bell please, Maisy."

Mom uses her mean voice.

Maisy runs inside.

She **throws** off her boots.

They hit the wall.

Then she runs down the stairs.

Penny runs down the stairs too.

I did not expect
Maisy to be this noisy.

I did not expect
Maisy to throw her boots.

I did not expect Maisy to run
off with my little sister, Penny.

"No running in the house,"

says Mom.

But Maisy
and Penny
are gone.

Chapter
Two

Mom and I wipe off the marks
Maisy's boots left on the wall.

Mom's **HARD** lips now match
her **MEAN** voice.

We hear Penny
laughing.
Maisy is
laughing too.

Mom gets to the kitchen first.

"Girls,"

says Mom.

Penny is still naked.
Now Maisy is too. They
are both holding two
cookies in each hand.

Maisy cannot talk. Her mouth
is full of cookie crumbs.

Mom says, "Those cookies
WERE for this afternoon."
Mom says **WERE** a bit loud.

Mom calls out to Dad, who is in the living room. "Can you take Penny to the park?"

"I am just reading the —"

"Take Penny to the park, **PLEASE**," says Mom.

Mom says *please* like she does not really mean *please*.

Mom says *please* like Dad has no choice.

Maisy burps.
Penny laughs.

BURRRRRP

Maisy picks Mom's car keys up off the counter.

Mom looks at Maisy. "Pants back on, and keys down," she says.

Maisy pulls on her undies and . . .

...RUNS

past us and out
the back door.

Mom shakes her head.

"Ginger, grab the broom so we can sweep up the cookie crumbs."

When we are done sweeping, I go outside. I cannot see Maisy.

"Maisy?"
I call.

"Maisy?"

The backyard is quiet.

I am Ginger Green,
Playdate Queen.
But I am all alone.

Maisy only got here
a few minutes ago.
Now she is gone.

I lost Maisy.

I lost my playdate.

I feel terrible. At school, I never even lose my lunch box.

"Ginger," says Mom. "Where is Maisy?"

"I don't know,"

I say.

Violet walks outside. "What are you doing?" she asks.

"Looking for Maisy," says Mom.

"You lost Maisy?" asks Violet.

"Not lost," says Mom.

"Just not found," I say.

"Crazy Maisy,"

says Violet.

"That is not
nice," says Mom.

"Maisy!"

I yell.

"There she is!"

says Violet. She points.

Maisy is way up high.
Maisy is up on our roof!

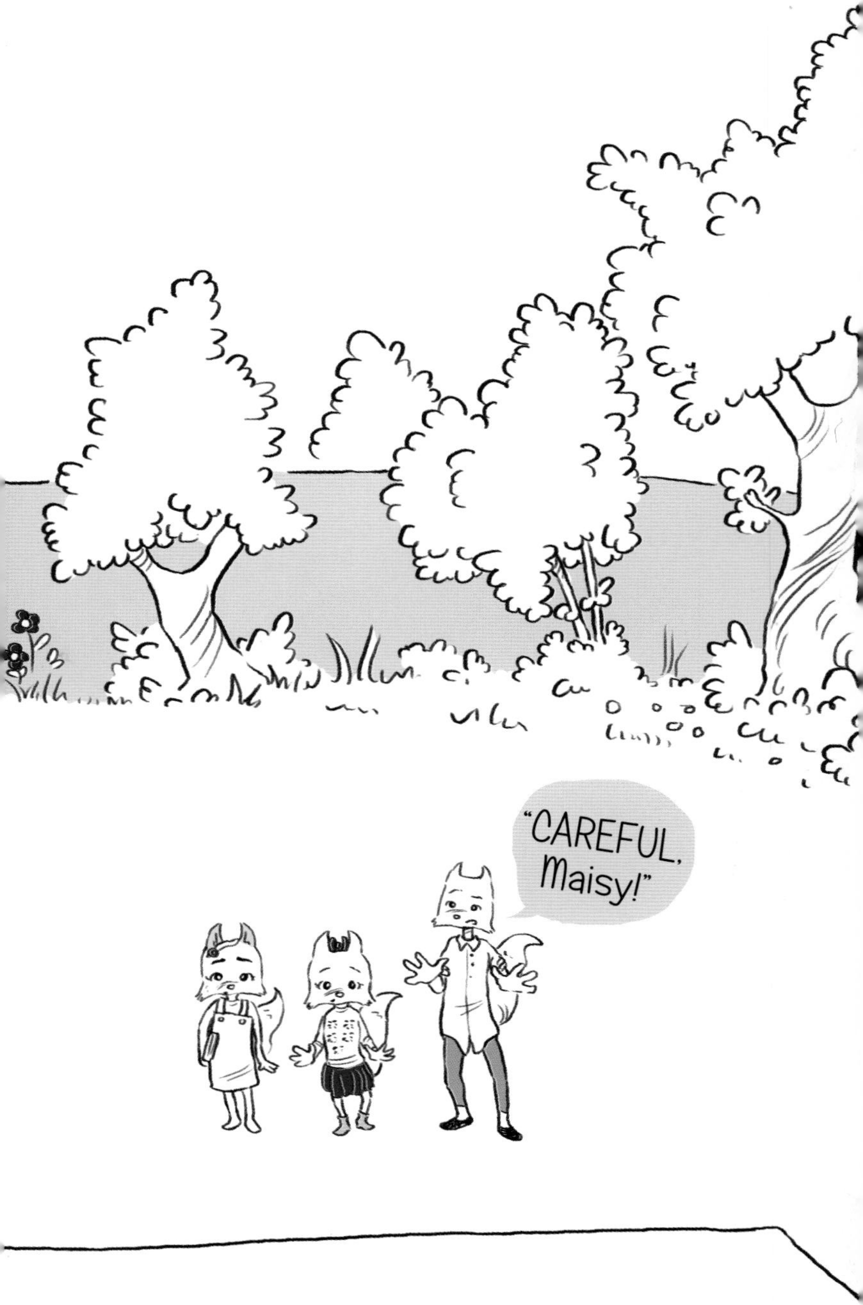
"CAREFUL, Maisy!"

Maisy looks happy on the roof.

Maisy looks very happy
in her undies on the roof.
But I am worried.

Maisy is up
very high.

"I didn't know Maisy was a climber," says Mom.

"I didn't know Maisy was a climber either," I say.

At school, Maisy does not climb. At school, Maisy is fast and loud. But at school, Maisy being fast and loud is fun.

Mom is loud now.

"COME DOWN!"

she shouts.

Maisy smiles. She is
holding Mom's car keys.

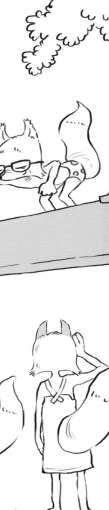

We hear banging.

"What was that?" Mom and
Violet ask at the same time.

Chapter
Three

Mom runs. Violet runs. I run.

The garage door is going up and down.

Maisy has the garage door opener on Mom's key ring.

BANG
BANG

I am **ANGRY** with Maisy.

Maisy is not naked at school.

Maisy does not eat all the cookies at school.

Maisy does not climb on the roof.

Maisy does not take other people's car keys.

"MAISY, CUT IT OUT!"

I yell.

"COME DOWN!"

I scream.

"COME DOWN NOW!"

Maisy looks at me. She stops
pressing the garage door opener.

"OK," says Maisy.
She climbs down.
Maisy is quick as
a flash.

"Sorry," says Maisy.
Her voice is quiet.

"I will get drinks," says Mom.
"Violet, stay here."

Violet sits down. She picks up her book. She starts reading.

I want to read too. I am Ginger Green, Playdate Queen, and I just want to sit with my big sister and read.

I DO NOT WANT A PLAYDATE AT ALL.

Mom brings out some lemonade.

When I feel better, I turn
to Maisy.

"Want to do handstands?"
I ask Maisy.

"Great idea," says Mom.

"Great idea,"
says Maisy.

"On the grass?" I ask.

"Great idea," says Mom.

"I can do them on the roof," says Maisy.

"The grass is fine," says Mom.

"Just kidding,"

says Maisy. "Look at me! Look at me!"

I look.

Maisy is standing on her hands.

"Look at me,
look at me!"

says Maisy.

Maisy is walking
on her hands.

I jump up.
I LOVE gymnastics.

I walk on my hands. Then I do
a back bend.

Maisy does a back bend too.

Maisy and I do
FLIPS.

We kick
our legs and
stand on our
hands again.

I do this five times in a row.

So does Maisy.

Then I lie back on the grass.

"I am tired," I say.

Maisy lies on the grass next to me.

"I am crazy," says Maisy. "But I am

never, ever tired."

I am Ginger Green, Playdate Queen, and I remember why I LOVE my friend Maisy.

Maisy is silly, and Maisy is loud.

Maisy never does what I think she will do.

Playing with my friend Maisy is fun because it is *always* a surprise.

THE END

About the Author

Kim Kane

Kim Kane is an award-winning author who writes for children and teens in Australia and overseas. Kim's books include the CBCA short-listed picture book *Family Forest* and her middle-grade novel *Pip: the Story of Olive.* Kim lives with her family in Melbourne, Australia, and writes whenever and wherever she can.

About the Illustrator

Jon Davis

Pirates, old elephants, witches in bloomers, bears on bikes, ugly cats, sweet kids — Jon Davis does it all! Based in Twickenham, United Kingdom, Jon Davis has illustrated more than forty kids' books for publishers across the globe.

Collect them all!